I SURVIVED

THE ATTACK OF THE GRIZZLIES, 1967

I SURVIVED

THE DESTRUCTION OF POMPEII, AD 79

THE AMERICAN REVOLUTION, 1776

THE BATTLE OF GETTYSBURG, 1863

THE GREAT CHICAGO FIRE, 1871

THE CHILDREN'S BLIZZARD, 1888

THE SAN FRANCISCO EARTHQUAKE, 1906

THE SINKING OF THE *TITANIC*, 1912

THE SHARK ATTACKS OF 1916

THE *HINDENBURG* DISASTER, 1937

THE BOMBING OF PEARL HARBOR, 1941

THE NAZI INVASION, 1944

THE ERUPTION OF MOUNT ST. HELENS, 1980

THE ATTACKS OF SEPTEMBER 11, 2001

HURRICANE KATRINA, 2005

THE JAPANESE TSUNAMI, 2011

THE JOPLIN TORNADO, 2011

I SURVIVED

THE ATTACK OF THE GRIZZLIES, 1967

by Lauren Tarshis
illustrated by Scott Dawson

SCHOLASTIC PRESS / NEW YORK

Text copyright © 2018 by Dreyfuss Tarshis Media Inc.
Illustrations copyright © 2018 Scholastic Inc.
Photos ©: vi: Paul Sawer/Minden Pictures; 116: Courtesy National Park
Service; 121: 4X5 Collection/Superstock, Inc.; 125: Stephen Saks/Getty
Images; 127: Thomas Mangelsen/Minden Pictures; 129: Courtesy Chuck
Bartlebaugh/Be Bear Aware Campaign
Special thanks to John Hechtel

This book is being published simultaneously in paperback by Scholastic Inc.

Library of Congress Cataloging-in-Publication Data available

ISBN 978-0-545-91983-8

10 9 8 7 6 5 4 3 2 1   18 19 20 21 22

Printed in the U.S.A.   113
First edition, October 2018
Designed by Yaffa Jaskoll

For Scott Dawson

CHAPTER 1

TUESDAY, AUGUST 8, 1967
GRANITE PARK,
GLACIER NATIONAL PARK, MONTANA
AROUND 9:30 P.M.

Grrrrawrrrrrrrrrrrrrr!

The enormous grizzly roared with rage. Its dripping jaws were open wide. Its dagger-claws gleamed. And Melody Vega was running for her life. Mel had no doubt that this bear wanted to kill her.

Just moments before, Mel had been sitting in the peaceful darkness, surrounded by the magical wilderness of Glacier National Park.

Owls hooted. Night bugs shimmered.

But then there were new sounds. Sounds that made Mel's blood turn to ice.

Massive paws crunching across the ground. Wet, wheezing breaths. Low, thundering growls.

Mel looked into the distance.

And there it was, the grizzly. Its silver-brown fur glittered in the moonlight.

Mel's body filled with panic. And before she could stop herself, she was running as fast as she could. Within seconds the bear was after her, its paws crashing against the ground.

Mel's heart pounded with terror as she sprinted toward a pine tree. It was small and thin. But it was her only hope for staying alive. She prayed that this grizzly didn't climb trees.

The bear was just one leap away when Mel launched herself into the tree. She gripped a low branch, kicked her legs up, and swung them around. But before she could start climbing, the bear was standing on its hind legs. It swiped at Mel with a giant paw, and the claws tore through the flesh of her leg. Somehow Mel ignored the searing pain, the dripping blood. She clutched the branches with her trembling hands, pulling herself up higher and higher, out of the bear's stabbing reach.

But the grizzly didn't give up.

It pounded the tree trunk, ripped away branches, and bellowed with fury.

Graaaaaawrrrrr!

The spindly tree shook, as though it was as terrified as Mel. And then, *crack*. The branch in Mel's hands broke off. She tipped back. Time seemed to slow as she tumbled through the air, twisting and turning, and screaming for help.

Down, down, down she fell. Mel braced herself for the crushing jaws and ripping claws.

No grizzly had ever killed a human in Glacier National Park.

Until tonight.

CHAPTER 2

TWO DAYS EARLIER
SUNDAY, AUGUST 6, 1967
LAKE MCDONALD, GLACIER NATIONAL PARK
AROUND 8:00 P.M.

"Mel! I have a question for you," said Mel's four-year-old brother, Kevin.

"Go ahead," Mel said.

They were on the beach outside their grandfather's log cabin. Kevin was perched on Mel's lap, gobbling a roasted marshmallow. Their campfire crackled. The lake looked purple in the moonlight.

"What's the most dangerous, most scariest, most fiercest animal?" Kevin asked.

"Here in Glacier?" Mel asked. She swallowed the last bit of her own roasted marshmallow.

Kevin nodded.

"A grizzly bear," she said. "But only if you surprise it."

Everyone knew that.

"What animal can beat a grizzly?" he asked.

"Hmmm," Mel said. She loved her little brother more than anything. But he could drive her crazy with his nonstop questions.

"What about a mountain lion?" Kevin asked.

"I doubt it," Mel said. She stared into the campfire.

"Wolf?"

"Probably not."

"Coyote?"

"I don't think so."

"I know!" Kevin said excitedly. "A wolverine!"

Those were ferocious animals that looked like little bears but were really a kind of weasel. Mel had no idea if wolverines picked fights with grizzlies.

Luckily, their grandfather was just walking down from the cabin. His work boots crunched on the rocky sand.

"Did somebody say wolverine?" he asked as he sat down next to them. "I once saw a wolverine steal a dead deer from three wolves. The wolverine was no bigger than a fox. But it had no fear. No fear at all."

Kevin jumped up off Mel's lap. "Can a wolverine beat a grizzly?"

"No," Pops said, shaking his head. "Grizzlies are the strongest. But I'll tell you this. Wolverines are fierce!"

"Like me!" Kevin said with a little growl. He bared his teeth and turned his sticky hands into claws. Then he fell into Pops's lap in a fit of giggles.

The sound rose up into the starry sky. And at that moment, Mel could pretend that this

was just another normal, happy vacation in Glacier.

But of course there was nothing normal about this trip. And Mel was sure she'd never feel happy again. Dad was back home in Wisconsin. He couldn't miss any more work this year.

And Mom . . .

Mom was gone. She'd died last December in a car crash.

Mel felt a stabbing pain in her chest, like her heart was cracking apart all over again. She stood up, fighting tears.

"Be right back," she told Pops and Kevin as she headed to the cabin. She didn't like anyone to see her cry.

Mel hadn't wanted to come to Glacier this year. But Pops said they had to keep up their tradition. They always came to Glacier for two weeks in the summer. Mom would want them to be here, Pops said.

Dad agreed. "You love Glacier, Mel," he reminded her. "I think it's going to make you feel better."

By *better*, Dad meant Mel would want to do something other than sitting alone in her room. That she'd want to see her friends, play softball, go bowling . . . anything.

But Mel didn't want to feel better. She didn't deserve to feel better. Since it was her fault that Mom was gone.

Mel pulled open the door to the cabin as her mind flashed back to that snowy December night.

Her friend Teresa had wanted her to sleep over. Mom said no because the roads were too icy for driving. Mel begged and pleaded. And finally, when the snow had stopped, Mom had agreed to take her.

They pulled out of the driveway. The skies had cleared, and the snow seemed to glow. Mom had started to sing. "Row, row, row your boat . . ." And Mel started singing along. It was one of their funny traditions, from when Mel was a little girl. Whenever they were alone in the car, they'd sing together. The dumber the song, the better.

They were still singing when Mom rounded a curve. The car hit a sheet of black ice. They spun around and around and around, then skidded off the road.

The driver's side of the car smashed right into a tree.

It was all over in seconds.

Mel sat down in a kitchen chair. Dad was wrong. Being in Glacier made her heart hurt even more. Because everything here reminded her of Mom. Every sparkle on Lake McDonald. Every breath of the sweet air. The song of every bird that sang from the pine trees.

This had always been Mom's favorite place — and Mel's, too. This cabin had been in their family for more than sixty years. Pops and his dad built the cabin back before Glacier was a famous national park packed with people.

Mel looked around. The cabin hadn't changed much since then. It was still just four small rooms and a porch. It had no electricity, no running water. They slept on cots, read by lantern, and collected rainwater in a big barrel. The toilet was in back, in the outhouse.

But as Mom used to say, who needed a fancy house when your backyard was one million acres of Rocky Mountain wilderness?

Look in any direction in Glacier Park, and you'd see something that made your eyes pop open wider — a turquoise lake, a waterfall tumbling down a cliff, ice-covered mountains soaring into the sky.

Mel wished she was back home in Wisconsin,

where she could close the door, turn out the lights, and try to forget.

"Mel!" Kevin bellowed. "Pops is going to tell another story! Come on!"

Mel took a deep breath and headed back outside. She didn't want to upset Kevin.

"Okay," Pops said. "I have a story about an animal way more frightening than a wolverine. To me, anyway. Because one of these nasty critters attacked me one night."

Kevin's eyes grew wide. He had climbed back up on Mel's lap.

"Tell us, Pops!"

"Oh, I don't know," Pops said, pretending to change his mind. "I don't want to scare you."

"I am brave, Pops! I am very, very brave!" Kevin exclaimed.

Mel cracked a smile and held Kevin a little tighter. What would she do without her loud, bossy pest of a brother?

"All right," Pops said. "But don't say I didn't warn you."

CHAPTER 3

"This happened a very long time ago," Pops began. "I was maybe ten years old."

Mel looked at her grandfather, whose face was lit up by the firelight. He had white hair, a matching mustache, and skin that was all crinkled, like an old map. It was hard to imagine that he'd once been a kid like her. But there was an old photo of him hanging on the wall in the cabin — little-boy Pops — with his buzz cut and freckles. He was proudly holding up a big trout he'd caught in the lake.

"I was walking through the woods," Pops went on. "Not too far from here, maybe a half mile up the lake. I was heading back to the cabin, whistling some silly tune, swinging my lantern. Not a care in the world . . . until I heard a noise just ahead, a noise I'd never heard before."

Pops leaned forward. "It sounded like this."

He clacked his teeth together. *Click, clack, click, clack, click, clack.*

"Was it an alligator?" Kevin asked. He loved alligators. Most kids had teddy bears. Kevin slept with the stuffed alligator their aunt Cassie had given him.

"Shhh," Mel said gently.

Pops dropped his voice to a whisper.

"I should have stopped or at least slowed down, or found a different route. But I just kept walking along like a big dummy. And suddenly, *wham!* Something whacked my calf. I never felt such pain in my life — not before or since.

"The animal ran off. I never got a good look at

it. I hobbled over to a tree stump, shined my lantern onto my leg. I saw the strangest sight . . . dozens of long black needles sticking deep into the meat of my calf. And of course I realized what creature had attacked me."

"What was it?" Kevin cried.

Pops raised his eyebrows at Mel. She'd heard this story a hundred times before.

"It was a porcupine," Mel said.

"A porcupine?" Kevin repeated, frowning. He crossed his skinny arms over his T-shirt. "Pops! A porcupine is NOT a scary animal!"

"Who says?" Pops boomed. "All creatures fear the porcupine."

Pops explained that porcupines had more than thirty thousand quills on their bodies. The spikes protected them from enemies — bigger animals that wanted to eat them. Each quill was like a small arrow. When a porcupine's attacker tried to take a bite, it wound up stabbed in the snout. And when a porcupine got mad or felt threatened, watch out. With one whack of its tail, a porcupine could deliver dozens of quills deep into its enemy's flesh.

That's what happened to Pops.

"My mother had to use pliers to get the quills out," Pops said, wincing. "Took her about three hours. I fainted once from the pain."

Kevin huffed. "I hate that porcupine, Pops!"

"Oh no," Pops said. "Don't blame the porcupine. It was just protecting itself. It warned me. That *click, clack, click, clack* was it telling me, 'I'm here! Please go away!' But I was walking around like I owned the forest. I showed no respect."

Showing respect in the wild. That was a big thing for Pops — and Mom, too. She was always reminding Mel that Glacier really belonged to the animals. "We're just guests here," she liked to say.

Both she and Pops worried that the park was getting too crowded. And some people didn't understand how to act when they were hiking or camping. It used to drive Mom crazy when people littered on the trails. Mom's temper could be fiery sometimes. Just like Mel's.

"Excuse me!" she'd yell, handing the person their empty soda bottle or Milky Way wrapper. "I think you dropped something."

"Tell another story, Pops," Kevin pleaded. "Tell about a wolverine, or a wolf, or a tiger, or an alligator . . ."

Pops chuckled. "Enough stories for tonight," he said. He stood up slowly. His stiff knees cracked. "Remember, Aunt Cassie's coming tomorrow. Right after breakfast."

"Yay!" Kevin said. Aunt Cassie was Mom's best friend. She always joined them for a few days in Glacier. Last year, Mel would have been counting down the minutes until Aunt Cassie showed up in her little red Volkswagen. But the last thing Mel needed now was another reminder of Mom — another reason to cry.

Kevin slid off Mel's lap and scampered toward the cabin.

"Race you, Pops!" he called.

"Put out the fire, would you, Mel?" Pops asked. Then he turned and started limping after Kevin. "I'm coming for you! And I'm bringing my porcupine with me!"

Kevin shrieked happily. They disappeared into the darkness. A minute later Mel heard the creak and slam of the porch door.

Mel doused the fire with water from the lake and used a shovel to pile sand on the smoldering logs. Even a small ember could drift into the woods and start a fire. There were already more than ten wildfires burning in the northern parts of the park.

So far, firefighters had kept them from spreading. But one windy night could change that. Especially in August, when the weather was hot and dry.

Mel threw on extra sand, just to be sure.

When the fire was good and out, Mel stood for a few minutes, leaning on the shovel. She stared up at the stars. She could see a million more here than back home in Milwaukee.

And that's when she noticed something strange ... the total silence. The owls had stopped hooting. The night bugs weren't buzzing. The whole forest seemed to be holding its breath.

And then Mel heard a twig snap. Leaves rustling. Deep, wheezing breaths.

The hairs on Mel's arms stood straight up.

She wasn't alone. Something was here.

Something big.

CHAPTER 4

Mel looked into the woods but couldn't see a thing. It was too dark.

She put down the shovel and pushed away her jitters. She had no reason to feel scared. There was no crime in Glacier. Pops didn't even have a lock for the cabin door. Their worst fear was that a skunk would sneak into the house and stink everything up.

Mel took a step toward the cabin.

And then she heard it.

Grrrrrrrrrrrrrrr.

At first she thought it was thunder. But the sky was perfectly clear.

Grrrrrrrrrrrrrrrrr.

Mel stopped, her heart pounding. Should she run? Stay still? What was out there?

She remembered Grandpa's story about the porcupine. Was this animal trying to scare her away? She swallowed hard and slowly turned to look.

She froze. The shape of an enormous animal hovered at the edge of the woods. A second later, it stepped out of the shadows, into a pool of moonlight.

Mel gasped. The creature had shaggy fur and dark eyes. But it was the hump that rose up between its shoulders that told Mel what it was.

A grizzly bear.

Mel blinked. It seemed impossible, like it had leaped out of Kevin's imagination.

Except that Mel could see it. She could hear it. And now a voice in her mind was screaming in panic.

Run! Run!

But somehow Mel shut out the screeching voice in her brain. She didn't run or shriek. Because if she did that, the grizzly would almost definitely come after her — and probably attack.

Mom had told her that. Over and over. Grizzly attacks were very rare. No person had ever been killed by a grizzly in Glacier. In fact, most people who came here never saw one, even if they searched for weeks. Still, Mom always wanted Mel to be prepared . . . for anything.

And so now Mel did exactly what Mom had told her to do. As the grizzly slowly rose up onto its hind legs, she didn't look it in the eye. She didn't want to make it feel threatened. With her eyes glued to the ground, she walked backward toward the cabin. Very slowly.

Out of the corner of her eye, Mel saw the grizzly drop back down onto all fours. She felt its eyes drilling into her. Its growls and grunts rumbled her ears.

Step by shaking step, Mel kept walking

backward. The cabin was only a few yards away. But it seemed like hours before she got there.

And then Mel couldn't stop herself. She turned and practically flew up the rickety wooden stairs to the porch.

She burst into the cabin and slammed the heavy wooden door shut behind her.

"Mel?" Pops said. He and Kevin were right there on the couch. Pops was reading Kevin his bedtime story. "What happened?"

Mel didn't say anything. She was looking out the small square window in the door. It was very dark outside. But there was just enough moonlight to see that there was nothing on the porch. Mel's knees went weak with relief. The bear hadn't followed her.

She spun around and locked eyes with Pops.

"I s-saw . . . a grizzly," she stammered.

Pops put the book down. "Where?"

"Right outside! It came out of the woods by the beach and . . . I thought maybe it followed me."

Mel saw the doubt on Pops's face.

"Are you sure?" Pops said. "Grizzlies don't bother with people. You know that."

"Of course I know tha —" Mel started, but Kevin cut her off.

"I want to see the grizzly!" He leaped off the couch. Before Mel could stop him, he'd flung open the door.

And there it was, standing on the porch. The grizzly was on all fours, staring at her little brother.

"Kevin!" Mel snatched her brother and kicked the door shut with her foot.

They all stood there for a moment, frozen in shock.

Mel couldn't help herself. She held Kevin tight and stepped to the small window. Pops leaned in to look, too. The bear was still there. It was pacing back and forth, sniffing the ground.

"There's something wrong with that bear," Pops said. "Look how thin it is."

Pops was right. The bear was very big. But its light-brown coat seemed to hang off its skeleton.

Mel could see the outline of its spine poking up through its fur.

Kevin reached out and knocked on the window.

"Hi, bear! Hi, bear!"

"No, Kevin, don't!" Mel warned him, grabbing his hand.

Too late.

The bear looked up at them. It slowly rose onto its hind legs. Then, with the speed of a striking cobra, the enormous bear lunged at the door. Its giant, clawed paw came smashing through the window right toward Kevin's face.

CHAPTER 5

Mel leaped away as the claws whooshed through the air, missing Kevin's cheek by inches. A shard of glass shot into Mel's arm. But she barely noticed the pain.

Her eyes were glued to the grizzly's paw.

The bear was reaching through the hole in the door, swiping at the air with its pointed white claws. Each claw was at least three inches long. Mel tried not to think of what those claws would do to her flesh. Or to Kevin's.

As if that wasn't horrifying enough, the grizzly

thrust its head through the window. Kevin shrieked and Mel stumbled back. The bear started bashing its paws against the old, rattling door. Its dripping-wet jaws snapped open and closed. A cloud of the bear's steaming breath rushed up Mel's nose. She gagged. It smelled like rotting meat and vomit.

Pops grabbed hold of Mel's arm and pulled her back.

"Go away!" he shouted at the grizzly. Mel had never heard her grandfather scream so loudly. And somehow it worked.

The bear pulled its head out of the door. There was a moment of silence.

But then, *BAM!* The entire cabin shook as the bear threw its body against the door.

Bam! Bam! Bam!

The wood of the door groaned and cracked.

Bam!

A lamp crashed to the floor.

Bam!

The framed picture of little-boy Pops fell to the ground.

Crash!

Between each slam, there was a skin-crawling scratching noise, like giant fingernails cutting across a chalkboard. The sound of the bear's claws digging into the wood.

Kevin was whimpering in fear, burying his head in Mel's neck. She held him tight. What would happen if the grizzly got inside the cabin?

Mel looked frantically around their small room, searching for something she could use to fight back. But it was hopeless. Even if they'd had a loaded rifle within reach, there was no guarantee bullets would stop the grizzly in time.

If that grizzly got in here, they were all doomed.

Suddenly, Pops snatched up their dinner bell from the table. It was big and made of brass. He shook it hard, right in front of the broken window.

Clang! Clang! Clang!

The sound was deafening. Kevin put his hands over his ears.

They stood there for one second, two seconds, five seconds, waiting for another *bam* on the door. But the sound never came. Mel held her breath. Pops stood frozen, still holding the bell high in the air.

A minute passed.

Finally, Pops lowered the bell and let out a big

breath. He peered through the broken window. "It's gone," he said.

Mel stepped up and looked outside. Pops was right. The bear was nowhere in sight.

But its deathly stink still hung in the air.

CHAPTER 6

"What do we do now?" Mel asked Pops.

He was cleaning the cut on her arm. The shard of glass had left her with a nasty, oozing gash.

"We need to tell the rangers," he said. "The station is closed now. But I'll call first thing in the morning."

"What will they do?"

"They'll have to trap the bear," he said, tearing open a Band-Aid and carefully pressing it over Mel's cut. "They'll move it up to the mountains, way into the wilderness."

He explained that the rangers had a special kind of trailer for trapping problem bears. They'd hitch it to a jeep and drive it to where the bear was last seen. They'd bait the trap with deer or elk meat. The bear would climb inside to get the bait. And then, *slam!* a door would shut behind it, locking it in. Then the rangers would drive the trailer up into the wilds of the park, far from the campgrounds and hiking trails. They'd release the bear and drive away.

"What if that grizzly comes back here?" Mel asked.

"It won't," Pops said.

But his eyes flickered, and Mel could see he wasn't so sure.

Mel wanted to help Pops clean up the broken glass. But Kevin needed her. The little guy was all shaken up. Mel found him on her tiny cot, tears pouring down his face.

"I'm sorry, Mel! I made the bear mad!"

"Oh, Kev," Mel said, lying down next to him and pulling him in close. "It's not your fault." She tried to make her voice sound calm like Mom's always did when they were upset. "You didn't do anything wrong. Shhhh, shhhhh."

After a few minutes, Kevin's sobs slowed down, and Mel pulled the blanket over them. She thought about all those times Mom's calm words made things better.

There was the time they saw bats in the outhouse. And the time they discovered a huge raccoon standing on the counter in the cabin. It had looked at them and hissed.

"Well, good morning to you, too," Mom had said to the raccoon.

She always made them feel lucky when they saw something wild. To her, a shiny green beetle was more beautiful than a diamond ring. Every spider's web was a work of art.

But Mom wouldn't have felt lucky tonight. That bear had terrified all of them, even Pops. In fact, Mel was secretly glad that Kevin wanted to sleep with her. She snuggled up closer to him. A few minutes later, he drifted off to sleep with both arms wrapped tight around Mel's neck.

Mel could hear Pops moving around the cabin. He'd already hammered a piece of wood over the broken window in the door. Now he was sweeping up the glass.

She closed her eyes and tried to fall asleep. But the bear attack kept playing over and over again in her head, like a slideshow that wouldn't stop.

It just didn't make sense. Grizzlies didn't act that way. Or smell that way. At least, no grizzly she'd ever heard of.

She'd only seen a grizzly one other time in her life. As Kevin breathed softly next to her, she thought back on that unforgettable day.

CHAPTER 7

It was two summers ago. She and Mom were hiking together on one of their favorite trails. It was just the two of them — Dad had stayed at the cabin to watch Kevin, and Pops's knees had been giving him trouble. Mel was always happy to have Mom to herself.

They were walking along a babbling stream when suddenly Mom gasped. Mel followed her worried gaze across the water. There, under a tree, was a large bear, lying on its side. It looked like it was sleeping.

Even from ten feet away, they could tell it was a grizzly — it had the hump between its shoulders. That was the main difference between grizzly bears and black bears.

It was important to know the difference. Because grizzlies were more aggressive and powerful than black bears. Grizzly attacks were very rare. They usually only happened when a grizzly was surprised or felt threatened. And this bear would be very surprised — and feel very threatened — when it woke up and saw Mel and Mom standing there.

How had this bear not heard them coming?

Mom and Mel always made noise when they were hiking. That was rule number one here in grizzly country: to make noise so you never surprised a bear. They talked loudly. They sang. They clapped. Mom and Mel were the loudest hikers in Glacier.

Why hadn't this grizzly woken up?

And then they figured it out.

"Mel," Mom had said, grabbing Mel's arm. "The bear is dead."

And that's when Mel noticed the bear's eyes. They were open wide, staring, unblinking.

They stood there for a moment.

"Come," Mom said. "Let's go see."

They crossed the creek and knelt down next to the bear. Mel's body jangled with a mix of fear and excitement. This was a once-in-a-lifetime chance to see Glacier's most fearsome creature right up close.

It was enormous, with shaggy brown fur dusted with gray. Mel studied the bear's rounded ears, its shiny black nose, the giant snout. Mom pointed out the bulges on the side of the jaw. Those were the muscles that gave grizzlies such a powerful bite — strong enough to chomp through metal.

"What a magnificent creature," Mom said.

She spoke very quietly, as if they were in an art museum. Or at church.

"It's very old," Mom said. "You can tell by its teeth."

The bear's mouth was open just wide enough to see inside. Its teeth were worn down and chipped. Three of its four long teeth — the canines — were gone.

Mel gently put her hands on the bear's side. They disappeared up to her wrists in its glossy fur. But what amazed Mel most about the grizzly — and gave her goose bumps — were the bear's paws.

They were enormous, practically like baseball mitts, furry on top, with thick black pads on the bottom. She knew how powerful they could be: One smack could knock out a moose. And those claws . . . long and white and slightly curved. Mel touched the tip of one with her finger. It felt as strong as steel.

Mom and Mel sat with the bear for a long time, until the sun started to drop down in the sky. Then they gathered as many fallen pine branches as they could. They laid them carefully over the grizzly's body. They said a little prayer. And they left the bear in its wild resting place.

"We'll never forget this," Mom had said.

Mom was right. Mel could still remember every detail of that day.

That grizzly didn't seem like a ferocious beast. It was beautiful, like one of Glacier's lakes or waterfalls.

Nothing like that monster they'd seen tonight.

CHAPTER 8

THE NEXT MORNING
MONDAY, AUGUST 7, 1967
THE CABIN

Mel woke up to the smell of eggs and toast.

Kevin was gone; he'd left his stuffed alligator tucked in next to Mel. Mel threw on her jeans and sweatshirt and padded into the kitchen. Kevin had finished breakfast and was busily drawing a picture.

"Look, Melly!" he cried. "It's a picture of me and my wolverine beating up that mean grizzly!"

Mel kissed his head and looked over his shoulder at his scribbles. Somehow Kevin had turned last night's terror into a thrilling adventure. She wished she was a little kid again.

Pops looked tired, too. Mel doubted he'd closed his eyes last night. But he smiled as he served her a plate heaped with scrambled eggs and buttery toast.

There was a knock at the door. They all jumped a little bit, before a familiar voice called out, "Hello!"

"Aunt Cassie!" Kevin said gleefully.

"Come in!" Pops answered.

A moment later, the door swung open and Aunt Cassie appeared. With her yellow-and-pink dress and her green suitcase in hand, Aunt Cassie looked like a flower — a six-foot flower with round glasses and an Afro.

Mel's throat tightened. The last time she'd seen Aunt Cassie was at Mom's funeral, in December. Aunt Cassie had written Mel about ten letters since then. But Mel hadn't written back. She'd never known what to say. And now she felt ashamed. She couldn't even look at Aunt Cassie.

But before Mel knew it, Aunt Cassie's arms were around her. "I've missed you!" she said. She put her hand on Mel's cheek so Mel had no choice but to meet her gaze. And to Mel's surprise, there wasn't even a flicker of anger in Aunt Cassie's eyes. Just the usual love and maybe a touch of sadness. Somehow, that split-second look between her and Aunt Cassie said more than one hundred letters could.

"And you, little man," Aunt Cassie said to Kevin. "You've grown at least a foot!" Kevin hopped up and hugged her around the legs.

"So . . ." Aunt Cassie said when Kevin finally let go. "Who wants to tell me what happened here?" She pointed to the cabin door. Or what was left of it.

The wood of the door was cracked, the hinges bent. There were deep scratches in it from the bear's claws.

"A grizzly came here!" Kevin cried. "It wanted to eat me! I was brave!"

Aunt Cassie looked at Mel and Pops.

"Believe it or not, that's exactly what happened," Pops said.

Pops poured Aunt Cassie some coffee, and they told her the whole story. Aunt Cassie listened with wide eyes.

"I've never heard of a grizzly acting like that!" she said when they were finished.

And Aunt Cassie knew as much about grizzlies as Mel and Pops did. Because she'd also been coming to Glacier her whole life.

Aunt Cassie and Mom actually met here as little girls splashing around in Lake McDonald. They'd told Mel all about the adventures they'd had together. The craziest ideas were always Mom's.

She and Aunt Cassie would hike all day to find a secret waterfall or fishing hole. Sometimes they'd get lost and straggle home — smudged with dirt and covered with scratches — as the sun was coming down. But of course that was half the fun.

Now Aunt Cassie lived in Chicago. She was a writer for all different magazines. She'd even won some prizes. Mom was so proud of her.

Mel moved her chair toward Aunt Cassie. Being close to her made Mel feel calmer. But she still shuddered as she pictured that grizzly's claws aimed right at Kevin's face.

"That bear . . . it was like a monster," Mel said.

"It sure was," Pops agreed. "There had to be something . . . wrong with it."

"What did the rangers say?" Aunt Cassie asked.

"Nothing yet," Pops said, clearing Kevin's plate. "I called earlier but there was no answer. They must be busy with the fires. I plan to stop by the station later. But first I want to go to town and get a lock for the front door." He glanced at Mel. "Just to be sure."

Mel looked at Cassie, then back at Pops.

"What if Aunt Cassie and I go to the station?" she said. "I can tell them what happened."

She wanted the rangers to do something about the bear . . . now.

Cassie's face brightened. "Sounds good to me," she said. "I'm curious to hear what they'll say."

"That's fine," Pops said. Then he turned to Kevin. "Let's go, wolverine boy. We're going to town."

"Ice cream!" Kevin boomed.

On the way out the front door, Mel eyed the deep, jagged scratches in the wood. It looked like a maniac with an ax had tried to chop the door down. And there was a tangled clump of brown fur in the corner of the porch.

Mel shivered, even though the day was warm, and followed Aunt Cassie out to the car.

CHAPTER 9

Ten minutes later, Aunt Cassie and Mel pulled into the parking lot at the Lake McDonald ranger station. It was just a small log building, about three miles from the cabin.

They waited in line behind a young man with a mop of brown hair and a beard. He was paying for a trail map.

When he was finished, Aunt Cassie stepped back and gave Mel a little nudge toward the counter. Mel stepped up. The ranger gave her a kindly smile. He didn't look much younger than Pops.

"What can I do for you, young lady?"

Mel felt nervous, like when her teacher called on her. But she took a breath and looked the man in the eye. "I live down the lake, in one of the cabins," she said. "A grizzly bear came out of the woods last night and followed me up to the cabin, and then it smashed the window and tried to break down our door and —"

The ranger held up his hand.

"Let me guess. Skinny bear? Light brown. Long claws?"

Mel glanced back at Aunt Cassie, who raised her eyebrows in surprise.

"That's the one," Mel said. "How did you know?"

"We call that bear Old Slim," the ranger said. "People have been complaining about him all summer. A real troublemaker. Been raiding campgrounds. Making a mess of people's garbage cans. Stealing people's food. Harmless, though."

Mel felt her cheeks turn red. What was this man saying? Hadn't he heard what she'd just told him?

"Harmless?" Mel said. "That bear almost ripped our door off the hinges, and . . ." The memory of the grizzly's paw only inches from Kevin's face flashed across her mind. She pinched her index finger and thumb close together. "And it got *this close* to tearing my little brother to shreds!"

Aunt Cassie put a hand on Mel's shoulder. Mel realized she was on her tippy-toes, leaning over the counter. She let out a breath and took a step back. She didn't want to be rude. But she needed the ranger to understand.

The ranger nodded. "That Old Slim's a real rascal. A few days ago he chased a couple of boys at the Trout Lake campground. Wrecked their tent. Bit right through some cans of chili. Ate a whole pack of wieners in one bite." The ranger chuckled.

"Excuse me," Aunt Cassie said, stepping closer to the counter herself. "I'm not sure what's funny about this grizzly."

Mel heard something over her shoulder and noticed that the young man was lurking just

MOUNTAIN LION

GRAY WOLF

GRIZZLY BEAR

BIGHORN SHEEP

BALD EAGLE

MARMOTS

MOOSE

WOLVERINE

inside the doorway, listening. Were she and Aunt Cassie making too big of a fuss?

"The rangers need to do something about this bear," Aunt Cassie went on, her voice rising sharply.

The ranger's cheeks turned pink. "There's nothing I can do, miss. I'm just a volunteer." He pointed to the symbol on his shirt and shrugged. "Most of the the rangers are dealing with the fires."

He patted Mel's hand. "I'm sorry you were scared, kiddo. But I wouldn't worry about that grizzly."

Mel's temper flared up again. Because she was pretty sure she *should* be worried.

"Can you at least tell us why it was acting like that?" Mel asked. "Do you think I could have done something?"

"I wasn't there," the ranger said. "But from the other stories, it sounds like this bear's just a little . . . off. Like I said, I wouldn't worry about it." Then he stepped back from the counter; he was done with this conversation.

Mel was fuming as they walked back to the parking lot. They were almost at the car when a voice called to them.

"Wait!"

It was the young man with the beard.

He hurried over. "You're right about that grizzly," he said to Mel, catching his breath. "It's dangerous. Very dangerous."

Aunt Cassie and Mel waited to hear more.

"And it's not just that one bear. There's a big problem here at Glacier. If something isn't done soon, someone's going to get killed."

CHAPTER 10

The man's name was Stephen Weiss. He was a wildlife scientist, studying grizzly bears. He worked at the University of Montana. He told them all about his work as they sat outside the snack bar of the Lake McDonald Lodge. It was the big hotel across the lake from the ranger station. Aunt Cassie had suggested that Steve join them for lunch. Because it turned out they had a lot to talk about.

They bought food and brought it to a picnic table near the lake. The water was so still it looked like a piece of light-blue glass.

Mel ignored her cheeseburger and opened up a bag of Bugles. She popped one of the cone-shaped corn chips into her mouth. They were a brand-new kind of snack and were all the rage at school this year.

"I want to know everything about the grizzly that followed you last night," Steve said. He'd pushed aside his burger and bottle of Coke to make room for a notebook. He scribbled away with his pen as Mel told him how the grizzly appeared from the woods and wound up on the porch.

"You did exactly the right thing," Steve said, looking impressed. "You stayed calm. I don't think that bear was going to attack you."

"But the way it rose up like that . . ." Mel said with a shudder.

"That's actually not usually an aggressive stance," he said. "Bears stand up on their hind legs to get a better look at things. But if you had run . . . or if it had gotten into the cabin, I really don't know. Grizzlies are unpredictable. But I'd say you're lucky."

Steve asked her how the bear looked, smelled,

and sounded. He was especially interested in the claws.

"How long were they?" he asked.

Mel thought for a minute. She stared at one of her Bugles, then slipped it over her finger. It looked to be about an inch long.

"Way longer than this," she said, holding up her Bugle-topped finger.

Steve nodded as he wrote. "That makes sense. Grizzlies use their claws to dig for roots and little animals under the ground. It sounds like that grizzly isn't doing much digging."

Steve asked her a few more questions and then finally closed his notebook.

"All summer there have been an unusually high number of reports of aggressive griz-zlies," he said, picking up his burger. "You're not the only one who's had a frightening experience."

"But why are the bears acting this way?" Mel asked. There *had* to be a reason. She gazed at the smoke rising over the north end of the park. "Is it the fires?"

Steve shook his head.

"It's not the fires," he said. "There have been wildfires in Glacier since before it was a park."

He pointed to their table, which was now covered with half-eaten burgers, crumpled wrappers, ketchup-covered napkins, and bottles of soda. "*This* is the reason the bears are threatening humans."

"Um . . . the bears want to eat our hamburgers?" Aunt Cassie said.

She glanced nervously at Mel. And Mel knew what she was thinking.

That sounded, well, a little crazy.

Steve shook his head. "Not exactly. The problem is garbage. Leftover food. There's trash everywhere in the park. On the trails. In the campgrounds. Dumped in ditches. It's become a bigger and bigger problem in Glacier."

Mel thought of Mom, hollering at people who littered. She pictured her tiny mother standing on the trail, in her red bandanna and peace-sign T-shirt, scolding a gorilla-sized man for leaving his empty Coke bottle on the trail.

55

Steve leaned forward. His eyes narrowed.

"Grizzlies are *eating* the garbage. Some grizzlies have almost stopped hunting and eating berries and plants. They're now eating garbage and whatever food they can find at the campgrounds."

Steve told them more about the research he'd been doing. And suddenly what he was saying didn't sound crazy at all.

"As part of my research, I've also been studying grizzly scat," Steve went on.

Mel tried not to smile. *Scat* was another word for wild animal poop. And it had become Kevin's favorite word. "I have to go make a scat!" he'd said yesterday morning as he ran to the outhouse.

But what Steve was saying was serious.

"I've been finding grizzly scat with glass in it, pieces of metal and plastic," he continued. "Last month the rangers found a grizzly near a garbage dump. It had starved to death. It had glass embedded in its teeth. It probably couldn't eat."

"How terrible!" Aunt Cassie said. Mel pushed away her food. She'd lost her appetite.

"It is," Steve went on. "Some of these grizzlies are really suffering. And they're becoming more and more dangerous to people. They don't want to stay away from us. They think of us as a source of food."

"So that's why the grizzly followed me last night?" Mel asked. "It was looking for food?"

Steve nodded. "I'm sure of it. And once it got up to the cabin, it could smell the food inside. A bear's sense of smell is even more powerful than a dog's. And it saw you all as a threat to its food. That's why it became so aggressive."

Mel felt chills. There were hundreds of grizzlies in Glacier. What if all of them started stalking people? How could they ever feel safe in Glacier again? Something had to be done!

"So Glacier needs to be cleaned up," she said.

"Yes," Steve said. "But there are other problems. Have you heard of the Granite Park Chalet?"

"Of course," Aunt Cassie said. Mel had, too. It was a rustic hotel for hikers way up in the mountains. Mom had always wanted to take Mel there. "Wait until you see the view," she'd said.

"Is there a lot of garbage there?" Mel asked.

She hated to think of one of Mom's favorite places being littered with trash.

"It's worse than that, from what I hear," Steve said, lowering his voice. "I've heard these strange rumors. I'm not even sure I believe them. I just know there's something happening with the grizzlies up there. And I want to find out for myself. I'm planning on hiking up there tomorrow."

"We should go, too," Mel blurted out.

Aunt Cassie raised her eyebrows. "That's a long hike."

"Eight miles each way," Steve said. "I'm going to stay overnight. You're welcome to join me."

Cassie looked at Mel. "You really want to go?"

Mel thought for a minute. She'd never hiked that far. And what if they saw a grizzly?

But Mel didn't waver. Whatever was happening at Granite Chalet, she wanted to know.

"I can do it," she said.

Cassie smiled. "All right. It's a plan."

They finished their lunch and gathered up their trash. The garbage can was already overflowing. Mel bent down and quickly picked up the wrappers and dirty napkins that were scattered across the ground.

But then she looked around and saw there was litter everywhere. Broken glass glittered in the dirt. Paper bags lay crumpled under tables. There were even straw wrappers floating in the air, like ghostly little birds. It would take hours just to clean up this one small area.

And that's when Mel truly understood all that Steve had told them:

It wasn't the bears that were the problem in Glacier.

It was the people.

CHAPTER 11

TUESDAY, AUGUST 8, 1967
GRANITE PARK, GLACIER NATIONAL PARK
1:00 P.M.

"Look there!" Steve said as they walked along the trail. He pointed at a hummingbird fluttering above a purple flower. The bird was bright red and barely the size of Mel's thumb. Its wings were moving so fast they were almost invisible.

"What kind is that?" Aunt Cassie asked. "A calliope?"

Mel squinted at it. She and Mom had a book with pictures of all the birds in Glacier. They kept a list of the ones they'd spotted. "I think that's a rufous."

"You're right," Steve said. "Good eye!"

They'd been hiking for three hours so far, with another two to go. The Granite Park Chalet was way up in Glacier's backcountry. That was the more wild part of the park, far from any road. The only way to reach the chalet was on foot or horseback — eight miles each way.

Every minute or so, Steve clapped his hands. "Hey there, bear!" he'd shout. "Hey there, bear!

"Good to let them know we're coming," he explained.

Clap, clap.

The sun was boiling hot. Mel's tie-dyed T-shirt was glued to her sweaty back. Her hiking boots were too small. Her pinched toes had stopped hurting; they were numb. But she didn't complain. This was a beautiful trail. It had taken them over cliffs and down into bright green

CANADA

GLACIER
NATIONAL
PARK

MONTANA

IDAHO   WYOMING

valleys. Now they were walking through a meadow filled with wildflowers. There were more colors here than in a jumbo box of Crayolas.

Mel took swigs of cool water from her canteen and munched on nuts and raisins that Pops had packed for her. He hadn't been thrilled that they were heading to a place crawling with grizzlies. But Cassie had convinced him they'd be safe. And he was as eager as they were to find out what was happening there.

As Mel walked behind Steve, she noticed a jagged purple-and-red line snaking down the back of Steve's right calf. Mel had never seen a scar that big or angry. Kevin would be fascinated. She wanted to ask Steve about it. But right now he was busy telling them all about what grizzlies eat in the wild.

"The grizzly is America's apex predator," he explained.

Clap, clap.

"That means it can hunt any animal it wants. And no animal wants to mess with it."

Mel smiled, thinking of Kevin again. He'd have about a million questions right now.

"They'll hunt elk or deer," Steve continued. "In Alaska, the grizzlies eat lots of salmon. They pluck them right out of the water with their mouths. But here in Glacier the grizzlies mostly eat plants — like berries."

Mel's mouth watered as she thought of the sweet, juicy huckleberries that grew wild along some of the trails.

"They also love marmots," Steve said.

Clap, clap.

Those were cute little rodents that lived underground. Sometimes they'd pop their furry heads out of their dens and whistle at people who walked by.

"I'm pretty hungry myself," Cassie said. "Right now I could really go for a nice, juicy . . . marmot."

Steve and Mel burst out laughing.

"Maybe we should stop for lunch, then," Steve said, pointing to a fallen log in the shade.

Steve took out a sad little jar of peanut butter and some cardboard-looking crackers. He eyed the thick roast beef sandwiches Pops had made for Mel and Cassie.

Mel handed him half of hers. "I'm not very hungry," she fibbed.

"If you're sure . . ." he said, happily taking it.

"So," Aunt Cassie said, swallowing a mouthful of her own sandwich. "How did you first become interested in grizzlies?"

"I've always been fascinated by them," Steve said.

"But why?" Aunt Cassie coaxed.

Steve took a gulp of water from his beat-up canteen.

"Who wouldn't be? Grizzlies are powerful, smart, and curious. They're a lot like humans, if you think about it."

Right then, he reminded Mel of Mom. Her eyes would get the same look of awe when she talked about bears and other wild animals.

"How did you get that scar?" Mel asked, almost without thinking.

Steve's face fell. And right away Mel realized she should have kept her mouth shut.

"Sorry, I . . ."

"No," Steve said. "It's just . . . well, it's one of those big, sad stories."

"We all have those," Cassie said.

Mel looked down and tried not to think of her own big, sad story.

She was sure Steve didn't want to talk about his.

But she was wrong.

CHAPTER 12

"I grew up about a hundred miles north of here, in Canada. My dad and I used to spend lots of time in the woods. One day, when I was thirteen, my dad and I were heading to our favorite fishing spot. We came around a corner and surprised a sow and her cubs."

A sow was a mother bear.

Mel's stomach clenched. She knew what was coming. Mel had heard gruesome stories over the years of hikers slashed and bitten and left half-dead by mother grizzlies.

"The sow went after my father first. Just slammed him with her paw. My father went down so hard. It was like he'd been struck by a sledgehammer. When he fell, he cracked his head on a rock."

Steve took a breath. "Then the grizzly turned to me."

Cassie's hand had crept over and was now gripping Mel's. They'd both stopped eating.

Steve explained that there's no way to know for sure what a grizzly will do when it sees a person.

"It's extremely rare for a grizzly to attack a person," he said. "It might make noise, growl, and whoof. It might stand up to get a better look. Or it might do a bluff charge . . ."

"What's that?" Mel asked.

"It's when a bear comes running at you, but it stops short, maybe twenty feet away. It's just trying to scare you."

"I bet that works," Aunt Cassie said, with a nervous laugh.

"That's when most people would run away, which is a huge mistake. You should just never, ever try to run from a grizzly. Unless maybe there's a tree nearby. But even then, it's risky. Because some grizzlies will climb."

"So what should a person do if they think a grizzly is going to attack?" Aunt Cassie asked.

"Drop down and play dead," Steve said. "That's what I did. The grizzly came charging toward me, and I could tell she wasn't bluffing."

"How?" Mel asked.

"She was silent. Her ears were pinned back. She wasn't trying to put on a big noisy show to scare me. She saw me as a threat to her cubs. And she was going to eliminate that threat.

"So I dropped down onto my stomach and glued myself to the ground. I clasped my hands behind my neck to protect it. The grizzly slashed my back with her claws. I was lucky I had my pack on, because it protected my spine from her bites."

Mel cringed.

"I stayed perfectly still and quiet as she bit and clawed at me. I dug my toes into the dirt so she couldn't flip me. I didn't want her to slash my face or crush my chest. The whole thing was over in less than a minute. When I finally got up, she and the cubs were gone. I was in pretty bad shape. The worst was my leg. She sliced it open with her claw."

He pointed at the scar.

"And my dad . . . it wasn't the bear that killed him. It was the rock he hit when he fell."

"Oh, Steve . . ." Cassie said.

"But there was something else . . . something almost worse than losing my father. Men from town went into the woods. They shot the sow. And her cubs. And that's the last thing my father would have ever wanted. He loved the wild. He wanted to protect grizzlies. He would have understood that the grizzly was protecting her cubs. There were tracks everywhere. We should have known to stay away. My dad shouldn't have died that day. And those bears shouldn't have died, either."

"I'm so sorry I asked you about that," Mel said.

"Don't say that," Steve said, reaching over and patting Mel's hand. "I didn't have to tell you. But it's good for me to talk about it sometimes. It's never good to keep sadness all bottled up."

They all sat there quietly for a moment. And then Steve stood up. He shook his head, as if he was waking up from a dream.

"All right," he said. "We've got about a mile left to go."

They put their trash into their packs and set out on the trail.

Clap, clap.

"Hey there, bear! Hey there, bear!" Steve called out.

Mel looked around, wondering who — or what — was listening.

CHAPTER 13

The last half mile of the hike was torture — a trudge up a steep hill. Mel was sure they'd never get to the top. But suddenly there it was just ahead: the Granite Park Chalet.

"Beautiful!" Aunt Cassie exclaimed.

The stone-and-log building looked like a fairy-tale cottage, only maybe a little bigger. It sat up on a rocky hill. All around were grassy slopes dotted with wildflowers and a few small pine trees.

They staggered into the lobby, a big airy room with a rough stone floor and walls made of logs.

All around them, exhausted but happy-looking hikers were lounging in big chairs.

"Welcome!" said a burly man from behind the front desk.

He introduced himself as Greg. He was the manager of the chalet.

He offered them cold glasses of grape Kool-Aid and directed them to their rooms upstairs. Steve was in a small room on his own. Mel and Cassie were next door. Their room was barely big enough for the metal bunk bed that was pushed against the wall. But it was bright and clean. Mel yanked off her painful boots and peeled away her filthy, bloody socks.

"Those poor toes!" Aunt Cassie said, looking at Mel's bubbling blisters.

"Good thing my feet are numb," Mel said with a pained laugh.

"Tough girl," Cassie said.

Mel slipped on her red flip-flops and peered out the window. In the distance was a jagged row of mountains. The slopes were still white with snow. It never melted up there, even in the summer.

Aunt Cassie came up behind her.

"That's Heavens Peak," she said, wrapping her arm around Mel.

"I know," Mel said. Mom had told her all about it.

She could almost imagine that it was Mom standing there with her.

Suddenly Mel felt that cracking-apart pain in her heart. She felt the flood of tears coming.

She wiggled out from under Cassie's arm.

"Be right back . . ." Mel said. "I need to go to the outhouse."

She rushed downstairs and went outside. She found a chair in the corner of the big front porch. She just needed to be by herself for a few minutes, to pull herself together.

But seconds later three noisy and sweaty men collapsed down in the chairs right next to her.

"Whew!" exclaimed a man with a bushy mustache. "That hike was killer!"

"I think my feet are going to fall off," said a skinny man with no hair.

"You won't be sorry you came here," said the mustache man. "Not after tonight."

Mel bent down to scratch a mosquito bite.

"I don't get it," the third man said. "How do they get the grizzlies to come every night?"

Mel froze. She eyed the men.

"I told you," the mustache man said. "They dump all the leftover food into a big ditch. It's out back, down the hill. And every night the grizzlies come. You can stand right on the back porch and watch them."

"Sounds like a good show," said the no-hair man.

"Wait until you see!" the mustache man gushed. "If we're lucky, we'll see a fight! Last time I was here there were two huge beasts, and they were fighting over something. I dunno, a ham bone I think. And they just started going at it, *wham, wham!*" The man smashed his fist into his open hand. "The bigger one was clobbering the little guy. I thought it was going to rip its head off!"

His friends whooped and slapped their legs.

Mel fumed. She wanted to tell the men how disgusting it was, to want to watch grizzlies fight over a bone. But she didn't have the guts. She got up and ran inside. She found Steve and Cassie standing in the lobby, looking worried.

"There you are!" Cassie called to her.

Mel rushed to them, nearly knocking over a rickety table stacked with old magazines.

"You were right," she said breathlessly, looking at Steve. "Something terrible *is* happening here.

They're . . ." She swallowed hard. "They're *feeding* the grizzlies garbage!"

"What?" Aunt Cassie said.

Mel filled them in on what the men had said. Then she looked around at the people in the lobby. Was that why they'd all hiked eight miles to get here? For the grizzly show?

Steve looked crushed.

"Those were the rumors I had heard," he said. His gentle eyes were suddenly flashing with anger and disgust. "I was hoping it was just some crazy story."

Cassie was fuming, too. "We have to do something to stop this," she said.

Suddenly, Mel had an idea. "You *can* do something," she said to Cassie. She grabbed a magazine from the stack on the table. She held it up. "You can write an article!"

Millions of people read Cassie's articles. Last year she wrote about a company that was dumping dangerous chemicals into a river in Montana. After the story came out, the president of the company was arrested. Now he was in jail.

78

"She's right, Cassie," Steve said. "If more people knew what was happening in Glacier, things could change."

Cassie seemed to disappear into her thoughts. Her eyes grew steely.

"All right," Cassie said finally. "I'll do it. But I need help."

"I'll share my research," Steve said.

"And I'll do whatever you need me to," Mel said.

"Good," Cassie said. "Right now we're going to learn as much as we can about what's happening here, and how they're getting away with it. We'll hike back tomorrow morning and I'll start writing. I'll call some editors and hopefully we can get this story out quickly."

Mel's heart was pounding.

Cassie would make sure the whole world found out the truth about Glacier. And then things would have to change.

Mel just hoped it wasn't too late.

CHAPTER 14

"So tell me, Greg," Cassie said, looking sweetly at the manager who'd greeted them earlier that afternoon. "When exactly do these grizzlies show up here?"

Mel and Steve stood behind her, with painted-on smiles.

They were pretending to be all excited to see the grizzlies eating from the dump. If Greg knew how they really felt, he might not be truthful with them. Mel felt like a spy.

"Oh, the grizzlies come every single night," Greg said, neatening a stack of papers on his desk. "They'll be here when it gets dark. We'll make an announcement."

"We've been hearing all about it," Steve said lightly. "I'm surprised the rangers haven't put a stop to it . . . and, uh, you know, ruined everything."

"Because isn't feeding wild animals supposed to be against the rules at Glacier?" Mel asked.

Of course it was. There were signs everywhere: DO NOT FEED THE ANIMALS.

"Oh, the rangers know all about it," Greg said. "There were three rangers here just a few nights ago. They were out there watching when the bears came. Didn't say a word to me. And besides, they know we have no choice."

"About what?" Steve asked.

"We have to dump our garbage out there. Because what else are we going to do with it? The park service gave me an incinerator back in June so we could burn our trash. But it was way too small. The thing broke after a few weeks. I kept asking for a new one. But they just ignored me."

"So the park service knows all about this?" Steve asked, a little too loudly. Mel gave him a little nudge. She didn't want Greg to get suspicious.

But Greg didn't seem to notice. "Sure they know. This has been going on at the chalet for years. The tourists love it. And the rangers know that. I'm just keeping up the tradition."

They thanked Greg and went outside.

They were barely out the door when Steve started to rant. He was seething with anger.

"Did you hear that guy? Doesn't he know how dangerous this is? They're hurting the bears. And they're going to get someone killed. The park service knows? This is crazy!"

Mel's own cheeks were burning, too. "How could he not realize how wrong this is?"

Cassie shushed them. "We have to stay calm. We have more work to do."

She looked around.

"It's time to find that dump."

The dump was right where the mustache man had said it was, in the back of the chalet, down the steep, rocky hill.

The big ditch was filled with bottles and cardboard boxes and cartons. The stink of rotting food rose up. It reminded Mel of the disgusting smell of Old Slim's breath when he stuck his head through the window. The sight of the garbage made Mel queasy. So she looked down at the dirt instead . . . and saw something else.

"Look!" she said. The dirt was covered with paw prints. They were everywhere.

Steve knelt down. "Grizzly."

He studied an especially huge one. It was twice the size of his hand.

"See how the toes are lined up straight," he said, his finger hovering over the print. "That's how you tell a grizzly print from a black bear's. A black bear's toes are curved, like an upside-down U. And look here —" He pointed to the five dots running across the very top of the print. "These indents are the tips of the claws."

"How many bears have been here?" Aunt Cassie asked.

"It's hard to tell without really studying the prints," Steve said. He peered around, then walked about ten yards to the side. "But it looks like at least five different adults, and some cubs."

They hiked down the grassy hill. Near the bottom, there was a small cooking grill and a fire pit. A sign said GRANITE PARK CAMPGROUND.

They all stood there in shock.

"They actually let people camp out here?" Mel asked, even though the answer was clear.

"The grizzlies have to pass right through here on their way up to that dump," Steve said.

"This just gets crazier and crazier," Cassie muttered, shaking her head.

Thinking about it made Mel's skin prickle with fear. A creeping uneasiness filled her chest.

Granite Park really was in the middle of the nowhere. The closest road or ranger station was miles away. And Mel knew there were no phones way up here in the backcountry.

If something happened — if someone got hurt — it would take a very long time for help to arrive.

CHAPTER 15

LATER THAT NIGHT

The sun dropped down behind the mountains, and the sky turned bright purple.

They'd changed out of their sweaty clothes and were now in the dining room eating dinner. The sounds of happy chatter and clinking silverware rang out around them. But the mood at their table was grim. Mel picked at her bowl of beef stew. She pictured it sitting in the dump, covered in flies.

They talked quietly about what they'd learned that day and who Cassie was planning to call once they got back to the cabin.

"I'm pretty sure *National Geographic* is going to want the story," she said.

Mel could tell she was itching to get started. Pops had an old typewriter in the cabin, for writing letters. Cassie figured she could have the article finished within a few days. But then it would be at least two months before it was published, maybe more.

Mel wished she could press a button and instantly send this story to people all over the world. But this was real life in 1967, not some science fiction story set a thousand years from now.

The dining room was buzzing with excitement. There were about thirty people here, including a family with little kids. They'd overheard Greg talking about the even bigger crowd that would be there over the weekend. "Every room is booked," he'd said. "We'll have people out in the campground, too."

How many of those people were coming to see the grizzlies eat garbage?

Mel didn't want to know. Thinking about it made her nauseous.

Dinner was winding down. The waitress brought them all fat slices of chocolate cake. But none of them took a bite.

A woman at the next table stood up.

"It's time for our sing-along!" she exclaimed.

People clapped and cheered.

Steve turned to a man at the next table. "What's happening?"

"It's a Granite Park tradition," the man said. "Every night after dinner. There's a sing-along."

Cassie groaned. "I have a voice like a screeching parrot."

Steve chuckled. "Bet you it's better than mine."

The woman started to sing, and everyone quickly joined in.

Row, row, row your boat . . .

That song . . . the last time Mel had heard it was that night, in the car. The night of the accident.

Mel broke out in a cold sweat. Her heart started to pound. She felt as if cold hands were gripping her throat. Everything around disappeared. Her mind seemed to snap.

"I . . . I'll be right back," Mel stammered, pushing herself back from the table and hurrying away. She rushed out the door and into the night. She wasn't thinking. She could barely see. She had no idea where she was going.

She sprinted wildly through the darkness. She ran until the sound of the blood pounding in her ears was louder than the singing voices in her head.

She collapsed into the grass, buried her face in her hands, and let the tears come pouring out.

Slowly the spinning stopped. Mel sat for a minute, trying to make sense of what had just happened. She felt dazed, like she'd woken up from a nightmare. She remembered hearing that song, how the room had started to spin.

This wasn't the first time this had happened to her. That her panic had sent her on a wild sprint when something reminded her of the car accident.

Once, at school, a teacher walked by and Mel caught a whiff of her spicy perfume — the same perfume that Mom always wore. Next thing Mel knew, she was a quarter mile from school, in the middle of a park. She had no idea how long she'd been there.

Another time she was at the supermarket with Dad, and she heard an ambulance scream by. It sounded like the ambulance that had taken Mom away, after the crash. That time Mel wound up a block away, sitting on a curb behind a bakery.

It always took a few minutes for Mel's mind to really clear. And now she realized she'd better figure out where she was. Steve and Cassie must be looking everywhere for her.

She was just standing up when she heard something. A low, gut-twisting growl.

Grrrrrrrrrrrr.

Mel froze, and then slowly looked around.

Suddenly she knew exactly where this blind dash had taken her. She was at the back of the chalet, just a few yards away from the garbage dump.

And just ahead, glowing in the moonlight, was an enormous grizzly.

CHAPTER 16

Mel wasn't the only one who saw the grizzly.

From somewhere behind her, back up the hill, Mel heard voices and clapping.

"There's a grizzly!" a man shouted. "The show's about to start!"

Flashlight beams lit up the bear, which was about twenty feet in front of Mel. Its eyes glowed green in the lights. And those eyes were drilling right into Mel. She didn't move. She didn't breathe or blink.

Stay calm. Stay calm. Stay calm.

She just had to walk away, get back to the chalet. Like she had the other night at the cabin.

But something about this grizzly kept Mel's feet glued to the ground. It was coming toward her without making a sound. Its ears were pinned back.

It was acting just like the sow that had attacked Steve. And Mel knew — in her bones — that this grizzly wasn't going to just let her back away. It saw her as a threat.

To its food.

That ditch was right behind her. The air smelled of garbage mixed with fresh food. The workers had probably already dumped some of tonight's leftovers — the bait, to get the grizzly to come for the "show."

The cheers and whoops were getting louder. People obviously had no idea Mel was down there. Their flashlights were pointed at the bear. The beams danced around, stabbing at the grizzly's eyes. She had no doubt that the lights were making the grizzly even more furious.

Stop! Mel wanted to scream.

But she was afraid to make a sound.

Her only hope was to drop down and play dead. She prayed the attack would be quick. She realized she had no pack strapped to her back. No thick hiking boots. Nothing to protect her but her light T-shirt and shorts. She thought of that scar on Steve's leg.

She had only seconds to decide what to do.

Play dead, play dead, she told herself.

But then she noticed a pine tree, in front of a big bush. She knew that grizzlies could climb. But most didn't. Should she risk it?

Before Mel knew what she was doing, she had kicked off her flip-flops and was sprinting toward the tree. The bear was just a few feet behind when Mel launched herself upward. She gripped a low branch, kicked her legs up, and swung them around.

Too late. The grizzly was right there. With lightning speed, it rose up and swiped at Mel with its paw. Its claws stabbed into her thigh, ripping open her flesh. Mel gasped at the pain. But she managed to pull herself higher before the bear could knock her down with another swipe.

Now the grizzly was even more enraged. The frail tree shook as the grizzly pounded against it with its paws.

Graaaaaaawrrrrr!

Suddenly a man shouted, "Wait! There's a girl in the tree!"

The cheering and clapping stopped. It became eerily silent. All Mel could hear was the bear's low, hissing breaths.

A woman shouted, "We need to help her!"

And then . . .

Crack!

The branch snapped, and Mel fell into the darkness.

CHAPTER 17

Mel fell through the sharp pine branches. They scraped and stabbed her as her body twisted and turned. She grasped desperately for them. But the fragile twigs broke off in her hands.

She landed with a jarring thud in the bushes, smacking her head hard on the ground.

She shook off the pain and sat up.

Grrrrrrrrrrrrrr.

The bear was just feet away. She could see its glistening black nose, the gleaming points of its canine teeth. Mel braced for the feeling of

claws slashing through her skin, jaws crunching down on her bones.

She gripped a long, sharp branch that must have broken off as she was falling. She sat up and held it out in front of her. A ridiculous weapon, that little stick. She wouldn't have been surprised if the grizzly had laughed.

Mel heard something rustling in the bushes right in front of her. Probably some terrified squirrel.

Voices echoed. "Mel! Mel! Where are you?"

It was Cassie and Steve!

The grizzly stepped toward her, its eyes burning with fury. Its muscles rippled under its shaggy fur.

The rustling in the bushes got louder. And then Mel heard a strange new sound.

Click, clack, click, clack, click, clack.

Before Mel even knew what she was doing, she had pulled the stick back and jabbed it into the bushes. The stick hit something, something big and solid. And then that something leaped out of the bushes. It landed on the ground between Mel and the grizzly. Mel's mouth fell open.

It was a huge porcupine. Its quills stood straight up, like metal spears.

The bear reared up onto its hind legs. It let out an earsplitting roar. Not of fury. The sound was high-pitched, ragged, almost a cry.

The bear was afraid.

The porcupine *click, clack, click clacked*, louder and faster.

Mel's heart thundered.

In that moment, everything seemed to disappear. The voices shouting her name. The footsteps closing in. The flashlight beams getting closer and closer.

At that moment it was just three of them: The grizzly. The porcupine. And Mel. Three terrified animals, alone in the wild.

CHAPTER 18

AROUND 10:00 P.M.

"It was my fault," Mel said, sobbing in Aunt Cassie's arms.

They were up in their little room.

Steve had cleaned and bandaged the wound on her leg. The cut wasn't so deep after all. The claw hadn't hit muscle or bone. Mel would have a scar, but nothing like Steve's.

And she didn't feel any pain. She just felt confused and angry. Mostly at herself.

It was her fault. That's what most people at the chalet thought.

"What was she doing out there?" Greg had shouted. "Stupid girl!"

Mel thought Steve — gentle, quiet Steve — was going to punch the guy.

"Don't you dare call her that," he hissed. "This whole place . . . what you're doing here. It's wrong. It's a miracle that she wasn't killed."

That shut Greg up. But the worst was what Mel heard as Cassie was taking her upstairs. They passed the three men Mel had seen on the porch.

"It was unbelievable," the mustache man had said. "A girl and a grizzly . . . and then a porcupine scares it away! You can't make this stuff up!"

They men had laughed, as if Mel had put on a show just for them. The memory of it made Mel sob harder. Cassie held her tight, rubbing her back.

Finally, Aunt Cassie pulled away and gripped Mel by the shoulders.

"All right," she said. "That's enough."

Her voice sounded stern. "No more of this. It is not your fault. The people who work here have been feeding grizzly bears! How could this be your fault?"

"But if I hadn't run off —" Mel started, but Aunt Cassie cut her off.

"No," she said, wiping Mel's tears with a bandanna.

"And another thing . . ." Cassie said. She gripped Mel's chin, gently but firmly, and looked her in the eyes. "The car accident. That's not your fault, either."

Mel stopped crying. She stared at Cassie in surprise.

"Yes," Cassie said, her voice softening. "I know that's what you think. I know that's why you won't talk about any of this, why you're not able to let go of that night."

Mel sat back. "How do you know that?"

"Because I know you," Aunt Cassie said, gripping Mel's shoulders. "And maybe I would have felt the same way if I was eleven, and my mother . . . my incredible mother . . . was killed before my eyes. I would want to make sense of it. I would want to know *why*. *Why?* And maybe I would think it was better to blame myself than to think there was no reason ∴ . . that it was just an accident."

Cassie gave Mel a squeeze.

"But it's not right. You must stop thinking this way. You know what your mother would say to you if she knew you were blaming yourself? You know how mad she'd be?"

Mel pictured Mom . . . her fiery temper. And to her own surprise, she let out a little laugh.

Not that it was funny. But it felt good to laugh, like taking a big breath when you've been under-water for too long.

A few minutes later, Steve knocked on the door, then popped his head inside.

"Everything okay?" he asked.

Cassie looked at Mel.

Mel nodded.

Cassie turned to Steve. "It will be."

They left the next morning, and were back at the cabin by three o'clock.

Mel asked Cassie and Steve not to tell Pops what had happened with the grizzly. Cassie didn't approve. But Mel convinced them that it would be too much for Pops. At least right now. She promised she'd tell him and Dad when they got home. The whole story.

But they did share with Pops all they discovered at the Granite Park Chalet. They turned their cabin into an office for Cassie. For three days, the sound of Pops's old typewriter filled the cabin.

The editor of *National Geographic* was waiting for the article. On Saturday, they all drove into town to mail it.

They stood in front of the mailbox and Cassie handed the big, fat envelope to Mel.

"You do it," she said with a smile. "This was all your idea."

"Let's do it together," Mel said. They each held one side of the envelope and pushed it through the slot.

They stood there for a moment, and Mel felt a rush of hope.

—

But that hope died the next day, when Steve came rushing to the cabin. And what he told them was more shocking than anything Mel could have imagined, and far more terrifying.

CHAPTER 19

SUNDAY, AUGUST 13, 1967
2:00 P.M.

When Steve first came inside he could barely speak.

He collapsed into a chair and sat there in shock. Mel, Pops, and Aunt Cassie gathered around him. Luckily Kevin had played hard all morning and was taking a nap.

Mel studied Steve's face. It was a jumble of anger and sadness.

He took a deep breath.

"There was grizzly attack last night at Granite Park, at the campground below the chalet, just after midnight." He spoke so quietly that they had to lean close. "A nineteen-year-old girl was killed. The grizzly dragged her from her sleeping bag. She had a friend with her. A young man. The bear bit him up. But he survived."

Mel's whole body started to shake.

"One hour later," Steve continued, "there was another attack. A second girl was killed."

He swallowed. "And it wasn't at Granite Park."

"Where was it?" Mel asked.

"Trout Lake."

Pops frowned. "But that's at least ten miles from Granite Park. There must be a mistake. No grizzly can move that fast."

Steve closed his eyes and took a breath. "It was a different grizzly."

"But, son, that can't be right," Pops said. "It's just impossible. Two girls killed in one night, by two different grizzlies?"

"I know, sir," Steve said. "But it happened. It happened. I heard from the rangers today. They're hunting for the grizzlies right now."

Mel clasped her hands together. She felt sick.

Pops stood up slowly.

"All right," he said. "I've made a decision. We're leaving here as soon as we can. It's not safe to stay." His voice cracked a little. Like when he'd told Mel Mom was gone, after the crash.

By Tuesday morning they had packed up, cleaned the cabin, and loaded the car. Steve came to say good-bye to all of them. He was staying; the rangers had asked for his help.

"They understand that this place needs some big changes," he said. "They're already starting to clean up some of the campgrounds. And they're going to do much more. So at least that's a start."

"But look what it took . . . those poor girls," Pops said.

Both girls were nineteen, and in college. They worked at Glacier. Just like Mom and Cassie had when they were in college.

"And the bears?" Cassie asked. "Have they found them?"

"The Granite Park bear was a mother with two cubs," Steve said, nodding. "They've shot that bear. Her paw was completely torn up, probably by glass. She had to be in pain."

"And the other one?" Pops asked. "The Trout Lake bear?"

Steve looked down for a moment. And Mel knew what he was going to say.

"It was the same bear that came here. I'm sure. Skinny, sickly. They shot it, too. That bear was also suffering. Its teeth were full of glass."

Old Slim.

Of course that bear wasn't a monster. He was just a sick animal, in pain.

Steve hugged them all good-bye. He said he'd visit them at home in a few weeks.

And an hour later they were pulling away from the cabin, with Cassie's Volkswagen following behind. She was coming to stay with them for a week in Wisconsin.

Mel turned and watched as Lake McDonald slowly disappeared, until it was just a thin line of turquoise in the distance. She rolled down her window and breathed in the sweet smell of pine. Some birds sang out, as though they were saying good-bye.

Mel whispered good-bye back, just in case.

Just in case they never came back to Glacier again.

CHAPTER 20

ONE YEAR LATER
AUGUST 5, 1968

"Here we are!" Dad said as he turned down the dirt road that led to the cabin. The car had barely stopped before Kevin flung open the door and rushed down to the beach.

"Wait for me!" Pops called out, limping after him.

Mel stepped out of the car and took a deep breath.

Dad came around and put his arm across her shoulders.

"Good to be back here."

And it was. It looked the same as it always did. There was their snug cabin with the big front porch. There were the pine trees. And there was Lake McDonald, the bright blue water shimmering in the late-afternoon sun.

Everything looked the same. But things had changed here at Glacier. They'd been hearing all about it from Steve. And they'd read Cassie's new big story in *National Geographic*: How one tragic night in August would transform the park forever.

The deaths of those two girls had transformed Glacier and other national parks in America. Campgrounds had been cleaned up. Granite Park Chalet had a huge new incinerator for trash. The manager, Greg, was gone. There were more rangers to patrol the trails and to follow up on reports of problem bears. Park visitors received a long list of rules for camping and hiking — to never leave trash or food behind in the campgrounds, to never feed the wildlife.

To show respect.

Some campers and hikers were following the rules. Some weren't. Mel knew that it would probably take years for some people to understand what it really meant to show respect for the wilderness. But at least now she felt some hope.

After a simple dinner of hot dogs and beans, all four of them headed down to the beach.

While Pops and Kevin built a campfire, Mel and Dad walked to the water's edge. They stood shoulder to shoulder and looked out on the lake.

"Your mother loved it here so much," he said.

"I know," Mel said. "Remember how she used to dare us to jump into the lake?"

"And how she made us climb to the top of the fire tower?" Dad said.

"And the time she caught four trout in one afternoon?" Mel said.

"And then bragged about it all summer?"

They laughed.

They talked about Mom all the time now. And when Mel felt that heart-cracking sadness coming over her, she didn't sit alone in her room. She found Dad. Or Pops. Or called one of her friends.

"Mel!" Kevin screeched. "Daddy! We're roasting marshmallows!"

"Okay, Kev!" Mel shouted back.

"He's even bossier than Mom," Dad said, shaking his head and smiling. "If that's possible."

With the fire roaring, Pops started up his stories. Kevin snuggled on his lap, clutching his new favorite toy. Only Aunt Cassie would know where to find a stuffed porcupine.

Mel looked around at her family. Her eyes started to water. She missed Mom so much. And she knew how happy Mom would be that they were here.

Mel didn't try to stop her tears.

Steve had been right. It was no good trying to hold things in. Running from sadness was like running from a grizzly bear. It would chase you. And it would catch you.

Mel was done running away.

KEEP READING TO LEARN
WHY LAUREN TARSHIS WROTE
ABOUT THE GRIZZLY
ATTACKS, AND HEAR MORE
AMAZING GRIZZLY FACTS!

A mother grizzly and two cubs in Glacier National Park

WHY I WANTED TO WRITE ABOUT THE GRIZZLY ATTACKS OF 1967

Dear Readers,

You might think that after writing this book, I'm hiding under my desk with my poodle, Roy, nervously watching out the window for grizzlies. But no. First of all, we don't have grizzlies in Connecticut.

And more importantly, working on this book taught me that grizzlies are not to be feared. They are not bloodthirsty beasts. They are magnificent animals whose wilderness habitats are under constant threat by humans. This book is not really about two terrifying animal attacks. It's about what happens when humans don't respect the wild.

I first learned about the bear attacks of 1967 a couple of years ago, when I was visiting Glacier National Park. I was actually on my way home from a different I Survived research trip, for my book about the eruption in Mount St. Helens, in Washington.

As my husband, David, and I were heading back to Connecticut, we stopped in Glacier. It had been a long-time dream of mine to visit this famously beautiful national park. We had planned three days of hiking and exploring.

It was in the ranger station bookstore that I spotted a book called *Night of the Grizzlies*, by Jack Olsen. As the author of I Survived and the editor of *Storyworks*, I am always on the lookout for ideas for books and articles. And so I snatched that book right up.

Was it smart to read about grizzly bear attacks

during a vacation in Glacier Park? Maybe not. But after reading just a few pages, I knew I had a topic for I Survived.

As always, I did an enormous amount of research to create this story. I read at least twenty different books. I watched videos, studied photographs and maps.

I also studied the true stories of people who had been attacked by grizzlies. In almost all of those cases, the person had accidentally surprised a grizzly in the wild. Several of the people had purposely approached a grizzly, hoping to get a photograph or a closer look.

And that's what made the events of August 1967 so shocking. The young women who were tragically killed — Julie Helgeson and Michele Koons — had not surprised or threatened the grizzlies that attacked them. Both had been sleeping in campgrounds.

But as scientists agree, the grizzlies cannot be "blamed" for those attacks. And of course neither can those two young women. Those attacks happened because those bears had lost their fear of humans. Years of eating garbage and leftover food had changed the bears' behavior.

The attacks of August 1967 shocked people across the country. Some people demanded that all grizzlies in Glacier — and anywhere else in America — be shot.

Luckily that did not happen. The park service recognized that Glacier and other national parks needed to be changed to make them safer for grizzlies and humans.

In the days and weeks after the attacks, rangers began to clean up the park. The park service fixed campgrounds so they were less likely to attract bears. They built garbage cans that even smart grizzlies couldn't open. They made strict rules about camping in the backcountry. Never again would they ignore warnings about "problem" bears.

I hope this book has not made you afraid of grizzlies. My goal was to spark your curiosity so you'll want to learn more. I also hope this book inspires you to want to help protect our wilderness and the animals that live there.

And I do hope you get to visit Glacier National Park at some point in your life. It really is a magical place. It's doubtful you will ever see a grizzly. But if you do glimpse one — from a safe distance — consider yourself lucky.

Lauren Tarshis

Until the 1960s, people driving through Glacier and other national parks often stopped to feed wildlife. This is now strictly forbidden.

QUESTIONS AND ANSWERS ABOUT GRIZZLY BEARS

Is it safe to hike and camp in areas where there are grizzlies?

Every year, millions of people visit places like Glacier and Yellowstone National Parks, and hike through "grizzly country." Bear attacks are extremely rare. In fact, a person is far more likely to get hurt in a park by tripping on a trail or getting stung by a bee. Still, there are important rules for sharing the wilderness with grizzlies. Here are the basics of bear safety:

- Hike in groups. Groups of three or more are best.
- Watch for signs of bears in the area, like tracks and scat.
- Make lots of noise when hiking — talk loudly, sing, and clap your hands. Whistling isn't a good idea because it could sound like an animal and actually attract a bear to you. Bells aren't a good idea, either.
- If you do notice a bear, stay far away from it (and all wildlife). Never approach a bear. You risk startling it if you go closer. Don't hike after dark, or at dawn or dusk. That's when bears tend to be most active.
- Pay extra attention in areas where there are thick trees or where you can't see around you. Make extra noise near rushing water because it makes it hard for bears to hear you coming.
- Check for warnings on trailheads. Talk to rangers and ask if there have been bear sightings. Follow all of their advice.

- Make sure people know where you are going and when to expect you back.
- Have your family bring bear spray, but make sure that your parents practice using it. Studies have shown that it is the most effective way to stop an aggressive bear. BUT bear spray only works if a person knows how to use it. The spray cans are tricky to use. And a bear spray can is only useful if it's easy to grab; never keep it in a backpack.

Today in Glacier and other national parks, people are given clear warnings about bears and other dangers.

How many grizzlies are there in America?

Before the 1700s, tens of thousands of grizzly bears roamed North America, as far south as Mexico and as far north as Alaska. Members of native nations and tribes hunted them and worshipped them. But during the 1800s, grizzlies were hunted and killed by settlers, farmers, and ranchers. By the 1960s, there were only about 1,000 left in the lower forty-eight states (that's every state except Hawaii and Alaska).

The American government decided that the grizzly bear was in danger of becoming extinct — that it could disappear from the Earth forever. It needed to be protected. And so in 1975, the grizzly bear officially became a "threatened" species. This meant the grizzly could no longer be hunted. Scientists worked hard to help it recover in the wild.

Today, there are an estimated 1,600 grizzly bears living mostly in Montana and Wyoming (including in Glacier and Yellowstone National Parks).

Alaska has the biggest grizzly population in the world: 32,000. That's because there is a lot more open land and far fewer humans in our forty-ninth state.

There are also about 15,000 bears in Canada for similar reasons.

A grizzly catches salmon in Katmai National Park, Alaska

What's the difference between black bears and grizzlies?

It's important to know the difference because grizzlies can be more dangerous.

Grizzlies and black bears can be hard to tell apart. Both can be black, brown, and blond. Grizzlies are usually bigger but not always.

The best way to tell the difference is that grizzlies have a hump between their shoulders. Black bears' and grizzlies' faces also look different from the side — black bears' profiles appear straight; grizzlies' have a dip in them, which is sometimes called a "dished-in profile." Grizzlies' claws and black bears' claws are also shaped differently.

One more difference: Black bears CAN and do climb trees. Some grizzlies do, but they are far less likely to.

Study these pictures to see the other differences.

Black Bear

Front claw

1–2" long

Tall ears

Straight face profile

Front track

No prominent shoulder hump

Short claws

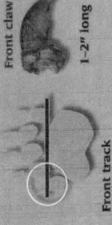

Grizzly Bear

Front claw

2–4" long

Short rounded ears

Dished face profile

Front track

Shoulder hump

Long claws

Photos by Chuck Bartlebaugh

What should I do if I surprise a grizzly in the wild?

You probably won't. Remember, grizzly sightings are very rare. And of course now that you know all the rules of hiking and camping in grizzly country, it's even less likely you're going to see one. But just so you know (because it's pretty interesting), here's what experts say to do:

- Most bears will not attack. So the most important and probably hardest thing to do is to stay calm.
- Do not run. This will cause the grizzly to run after you.
- Keep an eye on the bear, but don't stare it in the eye.
- Speak in a low, calm voice. This is so the grizzly realizes that you are a human.
- Walk slowly away, while still facing the bear.

Here's where things get complicated . . .

- If a grizzly bear starts following you, climbing a tree is not a definite escape — some grizzlies do climb!
- Sometimes a bear will charge you, as a "bluff." It is trying to scare you. But you shouldn't run. Most charges stop before the bear is very close.
- BUT, if the bear keeps coming, just before it gets to you, fall to the ground. Lie on your stomach, hook your hands behind your neck, and play dead.
- Keep your backpack on to protect your back.
- Dig your toes and elbows into the ground so the bear can't roll you over.
- If it rolls you over, try to get back onto your stomach.
- Be quiet and don't move. The attack should be quick and the bear will go away once it feels it is out of danger.
- After the bear leaves, stay still for as long as possible. If you start to move too soon and the bear is still nearby, it could resume the attack.

Is Glacier National Park cleaner and safer today than it was in 1967?

The events of August 1967 really did change Glacier and all of America's sixty national parks. But those parks, including Glacier, are still facing serious threats.

More people than ever are visiting America's parks; last year, over three million people visited Glacier, compared to about 900,000 in 1967. Bigger crowds mean more garbage, more noise, and more pollution from cars, motorcycles, and RVs.

Another serious problem is climate change, which is making summers hotter and drier, especially out west. This is causing bigger and more frequent wildfires throughout the west.

America's national parks are treasures. Park rangers work hard to protect the animals that live there and the people who visit. We all need to work together — and speak out — to make sure our national parks get the attention they need and deserve.

How can kids help protect the wilderness and the animals that live there?

This might seem like a strange answer, but here it is: Don't buy bottled water or use plastic grocery bags. Why? Because when you throw away a plastic water bottle or a plastic bag, there's a good chance that it is going to wind up in the wilderness or in the ocean.

Because that's where a huge amount of our trash winds up.

An estimated eight million tons of plastic are swept into oceans every single year. Right now, in the Pacific Ocean, there is an island of plastic that is at least as big as the state of Texas.

It's horrifying to think about what all this plastic is doing to fish, dolphins, whales, and birds. Plastic bags and straws end up in forests, streams, and rivers, where they harm animals, including birds and fish.

But here's the hopeful news: You can help solve this problem by avoiding plastic whenever you can. Here are some simple steps you and your family can take:

- Stop using plastic bags and buying bottled water. Instead, use reusable shopping bags, and get yourself a great-looking reusable water bottle to carry with you.
- Band together with your friends, teachers, and parents and encourage your school cafeteria to not use plates or utensils that get thrown away.
- Don't buy single-sized servings of chips and cookies; they create too much waste.
- Learn more about recycling. Some plastic can be recycled.

FOR FURTHER LEARNING AND INSPIRATION

To learn more about grizzlies and bear safety:

Get Bear Smart Society, bearsmart.com

National Park Service, nps.gov/subjects/bears /safety.htm

To learn more about protecting animals and the environment:

The World Wildlife Fund, worldwildlife.org

The Nature Conservancy, natureconservancy.org

To learn more recycling and creating less garbage:

National Institute of Environmental Health Sciences, kids.niehs.nih.gov/topics/reduce/

SELECTED BIBLIOGRAPHY

Bear Attacks: Their Causes and Avoidance, by Stephen Herrero, Revised Edition, Lyons Press, 2002

Bearman: Exploring the World of Black Bears, by Laurence Pringle, Charles Scribner's Sons, 1989

Fate Is a Mountain, by Mark W. Parratt, Sun Point Press, 2009

Glacier National Park: The First 100 Years, by C. W. Guthrie, Farcountry Press, 2008

Glacier Park's Night of the Grizzlies, DVD, KUFM TV/Montana PBS, 2010

Mark of the Grizzly, by Scott McMillion, Second Edition, Lyons Press, 2011

Night of the Grizzlies, by Jack Olsen, Homestead
    Publishing, 1996

*Pictures, a Park, and a Pulitzer: Mel Ruder and the
    Hungry Horse News*, by Tom Lawrence,
    Farcountry Press, 2003

*When Bears Whisper, Do You Listen? Expert
    Techniques for Viewing Bears and Negotiating
    Close Encounters*, by Stephen F. Stringham,
    WildWatch Publications, 2009